FIRST TUESDAY POF

CW00507298

Family
& Other
Haiku

Ralph W Osgood II

i

Copyright © 2024 Ralph W Osgood II

All rights reserved.

ISBN-13: 9798224901807

DEDICATION

Gloria in excelsis Deo

FORWARD

The volume you have before you is my third book of poetry. The poems selected are more personal than those of the first two volumes and are reflections from my life and about the people I love. I cover birthdays, anniversaries, and other events or memories growing out of life's experiences. You will find within references to my wife, my children, my grandchildren, and my parents - not only family, but friends I consider as family. And though they may be specific to me, my hope is that they will resonate from the human condition and in which you can find a universal parallel.

I have included a separate section of poems that use the haiku form (or haiku like). It is a form that I have come to treasure for the challenge of distilling a picture through words that total only seventeen syllables in its entirety. Usually a haiku has a focus on nature in the world around us. And those I do have, but I also fashion some around a thought or a comment, all under the sway and cover of the One I love most, my Lord Jesus Christ.

As in my other two volumes it is my fervent hope that they will speak to you.

RWOz2

TABLE OF CONTENTS

<u>Family</u>

A Mind 3

Cinderella Sliver 5

The One I Love 7

I Watch You in Silence 9

A World in My Arms 13

Look at Me Daddy 15

My Pure One 19

All Hail Eloise 23

A 39th Birthday Poem 27

For My Wife on her birthday 31

Mother's Day 1992 35

Twenty Years 37

We Are His Valentines 38

Look into my Heart 39

Silvered Hair 41

And Then There Were Three 43

Poem for a Grand Daughter 45

Crumb Crunchers 47

Come with Me, Grandpa 51

Come with Me, Grand Son 53

Beloved Husband 57

Three Months to Live 59

Driveway Tea 63

Fall Has Fallen 67

The Mockery of Falling Leaves 69

For My Friend John 73

My Mind 77

what does it signify? 79

Time Runs Quickly 81

& Other Haiku

M D Haiku 85

A Day at the Beach 87

Screaming Red 89

Smudge of Smoky Gray 91

Gutter 93

Snow Hush 95

le mot juste 97

My Pronouns 99

Not a Hurricane 101

Found in God 103

Obedience 105

love LOVE 107

Poured Out 109

There is none 111

Back Matter

Closing Quote 112

Watch for my next publication 113

ALSO BY THE SAME AUTHOR 114

About the Publisher 116

Author bio 118

Family

A MIND

What would you find inside a mind?

Some groups of facts of every kind;

A cluttered brain of useful things,

The something that to one will bring

To mind the data that was placed,

Inside the mind around some place;

But useless facts always remain,

For those we readily retain.

RWOz2

(Age 15)

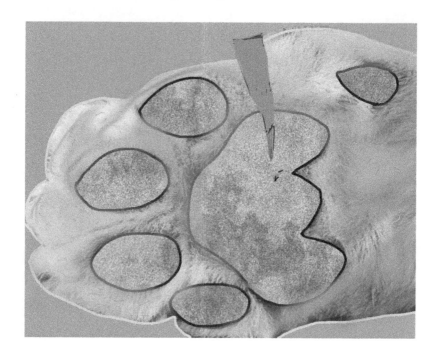

CINDERELLA SLIVER

Tell me a tale

    Of a lion and a mouse

And the outcome

    Of one big splinter

Of the gratitude

    To the lesser from the greater

And how each in his turn

    Saved the other.

In our own story

    We have a like tale

Of something

    That brought us together

For without a sliver

    I would have remained an "I"

        You … a "you"

But because of it

We are a "we" together.

THE ONE I LOVE

The one I love
 Loves the sea
Down by its roaring edge
 She likes to be teased.
She joyously dances
 Over each wave that advances
Watching curl upon curl
 Unfurl and unfurl.
Now don't think it odd
 I think she is at play with God.

For the one I love
 Loves the sea
And from its roaring edge
 She smiles her love to me.

I WATCH YOU IN SILENCE

I watch you in silence
 Speaking only in my mind
Counting up the treasures
 That are mine
Because you're my bride.

And although the hour is early
 And time for you to slumber on
I am awake beside you
 Framing thoughts
Of the future of we two.

Not just these days
 That run to tomorrow
For in them we'll be
 Imperfect still.

But of that thrill
 When we stand before Him
The self
 All given away
And made perfect in His Day.

To that end

    Let us live

Right choices

    Unheeding

Other voices

Knowing

    Who we'll be in that day

No furrowed worries

    The tears all wiped away

A smile in bloom for all around us

    And everywhere love at play.

A WORLD IN MY ARMS

Nothing else will focus your heart

Like the gift of a baby

Resting on your chest.

The sight of those tiny arms

Tells you, you are blest,

And stirs a love that's

Lasting.

You will know peace

With each trusting breath

You will know joy

Surpassing.

LOOK AT ME DADDY

"Look at me, Daddy!"
  She said with a thrill
As she set her two-wheeler
  To go down the big hill.
She inched down the drive
  Past the point of the bump
(So that bicycle seat
  Would not give her a thump).
Straight down the path
  Between the gravelly ruts,
O'er the leveler grass
  Now burnt into tufts.
All the way to the level
  She sat tall in her glide
While her long golden hair
  Swished side to side.

Just a moment in time
  Now in my mind fore'er etched
Left me musing on the porch
  After the words perfect to sketch
All I was feeling inside.

Then, from above my head

   And down into my view

A perfectly dazzling and golden

   Exquisite butterfly flew.

So tiny, so fragile

   Alive only a day,

Yet spreads beauty around her

   As she goes on her way.

MY PURE ONE

How I love your name

And the warmth it breathes o'er me

Yet I must confess

I am more enchanted

By your name second-given

Not the name of a barmaid - No!

But the all knowing choice

Of a wise father king

For his princess second-born

My fair Eloise

Eloise - in battle famous

Though to you it may bring a blush

At its echo - angels hush…

And lean nearer…

        Waiting…

          Hopeful

To be caught up in the music elven-made

Rising from some sylvan glade

In anviled notes of silver laughter

Whispering in my ear

In the silence after

The name of

Ma chère Eloise.

ALL HAIL ELOISE

Let us sing of my pure one -

    Famous in battle

Let us take up her praise upon our lips

    For 'tis fitting that we praise -

    Our lips and not her own.

With firm and measured tread

    She takes the Safeway, the Thriftway

    The thronging WinCo aisle

Swiftly to the fray she sweeps

    Where each combatant must join the list

    Against the exacting foe.

    (All buttoned and be-ribboned

    Anxious to take its toll)

With each stroke of the infernal engine

    The cents into dollars count

Pressing hard 'gainst the family purse and budget

    As to the skies they mount

Thirty-seven point eighty blink the lights azure

Thirty-seven dollars and eighty cents

    A princely sum that's sure

Yet is her brow disturbed?

    -No! There is only more resolve.

For her weapons this moment sheathed

    Leap out at the total called.

And 37.80 ceases flashing

    From its lofty height it tumbles down.

    First fifty cents are taken off

    Then six dollars in a lump

    Double the sum of forty

    As the coupons fall like trump

The total is hacked in half

    And as the haze is cleared away

    Another sixth is shorn

The total mortifies in rigor at 13.64

All hail Eloise

    As she leaves the field

    The victor undisputed

All hail Eloise

    Her booty gained

    In battle well-reputed.

A 39TH BIRTHDAY POEM

Today the clocks stop
 And the calendars freeze
And those chaps down in Greenwich
 Can all take their ease.

Leastways, as concerning
 This most recent rage
 The topic? - Let's drop it!
 No more of my age.

No more to grow older
 Why I simply refuse!
I have plenty things else
 About which to amuse.

So remember -
 As Father Time passes
  With gifts on his plate
 Wrinkles and lines
  And gray hair for your pate
 Just say, 'No thank you!
  'I'll not have any more.'
 And know you can do it

Check your Jack Benny lore.

FOR MY WIFE ON HER BIRTHDAY

Not many know you like I do

That sweet knowledge is mine alone

For like a pocket to a shirt

So my heart on yours is sewn

True, I sometimes forget about ketchup

And syrup and such

When I pour them on

You turn and chide me

- But never too much.

For it's when I think

(Without thinking)

That the one I like best

Likes what I like too

So, please, don't be insulted

When I bracket the things

I like with you.

Not many see the treasure

That is by my side each day

Few, indeed, know the pleasure

Of your impish teasing way.

Thirty-seven years of age

And sixteen of them with me

Three kids, two homes, four cars

An apartment on an alley.

So it should be with a life

That is shared

Only we two can remember

As we celebrate together

On this joyous day in December.

First Tuesday Poetry: Family & Other Haiku

MOTHER'S DAY 1992

Today's a day
 Like any other
The sun will shine
 The birds will sing

But this day
 Not like any other
We set aside
 To sing your praise

For your strength
 For your wisdom
For your love
 We thank you now

All these things
 You give your family
Every day
 Come rain or shine
Now we rise and
 Call you blessed
And I'm grateful
 You are mine.

TWENTY YEARS

Twenty years
  You and me
I wonder how the next twenty
  Will be

Full of splendor
  Just like the past
Full of content
  That will last and last

Full of hope
  For each new day
Full of joy
  That won't go away

All from the Lord
  The great Giver of Life
The One who gave me
  My beautiful wife.

WE ARE HIS VALENTINES

On this day

Show me someone

To show them Your love

On this day.

On this day

Show me the one

With room in his heart

For You this day.

LOOK INTO MY HEART

Look into my heart

See the gladness there

For my world is in your smile

All praise to Him

Who revealed His Heart

Joy radiates from There

And eternity in His Smile.

SILVERED HAIR

You can have your gold

On its looks, I'm not sold

Give me silver and its gleam

That - I whole-heartily esteem

But if you think

        This whim strange

Your opinion

        I seek to change

For God Himself

        Gives His approbation

On His saints

        In silver acclamation

Render to them your praise

        Fitting their renown

As complement to the Lord's

        Silver crown.

[Proverbs 16:31]

AND THEN THERE WERE THREE

First came a smiling daughter

A treasure for my wife and me

Then came the gift of a son

To complete our small family

Until in danced one more daughter

And then there were three.

Then came the leaving and cleaving

For the deep felt romantic,

For the noble and true,

For the fountain bubbling and free.

And now news for thanksgiving,

Clearly a daughter grand

Now news for rejoicing,

Praise for a son also grand.

And wonder for what hero will be

And again there will be three.

POEM FOR A GRAND DAUGHTER

She shall know Wonder

By her father's love

She shall know Joy

In her mother's arms

Through eyes now open

To a mind fresh and pure

Guard her now, father

May such she always be

Nurture her, mother

Both her soul and body

Come a day beyond tomorrow

When she stands on her own

Then she will walk steady

And never alone

For she shall know Wonder

And she shall know Joy

By the One who bids us

"Come and enjoy."

CRUMB CRUNCHERS

Crumb crunchers

So dear to me

Thumb suckers

Cling to my knee

Who knows

What I'll find

In my pockets?

While guarding

Their fingers

From power sockets

I am the

Tickle monster

Who ekes out

Giggles galore

When up-turned faces

Beg for more

I toddle among

These

Knuckle gummers

Whose mouths

Have a date

Across the summers

Here and there

They osmose

The wide world

With their tongues

Tis the age and

Time to whet

Their palates

So they'll know

The uniqueness

Of His Word

Through the sweetness

Of the honeycomb

So that in time

To come

They shall not depart

From Him.

COME WITH ME, GRANDPA

Come with me, Grandpa

Let's go and explore

Me you can follow

I'll go on before

Stay right behind me

Try not to get lost

Let's take this path

That other is blocked.

We will blaze a trail

Of discovery

What will we find?

Silly,

We won't know

'til there finally.

Look there a snail

On the bark of that pine.

Shh! Walk quietly

To get to that spot

A squirrel has a home

Where the tree had a knot

Boost me up on your knee

I'll have a look-see

A squirrel I seek

But all I see is a beak!

What do you know?

Some unmelted snow

Down hill we'll slide

Then get up and go.

Or we can make snowballs

Before tumbling up?

Act-chu-al-ly

Can I fill my cup?

It's so white and bright

So cool, so soft

It reminds me of home

And my little loft.

Then with arms up lifted

Through a yawn he said

"Grandpa,

Can you carry me?

And tuck me snug in my bed?"

COME WITH ME, GRAND SON

Come with me, grand son

Take hold of my hand

And together we'll follow

Him who is more than a man

We've a day fresh before us

Unsullied by sin

His face we'll look for

In the midst of the din.

Begin by listening

To Him in His Word.

Do not fear

And do not worry

You will hear

Him say now and again

Despite what you see

Despite what you feel

Despite what some say

Or would have you believe

He holds tomorrow

So no need to obsess

On that score.

And with trust

we'll lean in

As He goes on before.

BELOVED HUSBAND

Beloved husband

Of one wife

Beloved father

Grand and great grand

Beloved friend

To all in his orbit

Stillness now covers

The frenetic pace

Time is run out here

And begun elsewhere

Rounded third base

And now safe at home

Beyond the hurley burley

Beyond our view

Under restful skies

By the side of the Eternal

Father and Husband

And Friend.

THREE MONTHS TO LIVE

Three months to live

A wince

As the thought

Sinks in

Not for yourself

At the first

But for the

Beloved kin

So hollow

So gaunt

Not at all

Like him.

Now the vigil

Hold his hand

His skin to

Our skin

So silent

Pass the moments

As we pray

For him

And he knows

We are there

Though the light

Grows dim

Now, no longer

With us

But with his

Beloved Evelyn.

DRIVEWAY TEA

The trees have turned their coats

From green to crimson gold.

And soon like careless teens

Will drop them on the floor

And there they will lie

While I them spy

Safe and dry indoors

At this turn of seasons

Deciduous lesions

Steep the seeping rain

Into a spot

Of driveway tea

This cold brew

A fusion of leaf

And rain and dew

A concoction

Sans relief

Leaves a stain

Beyond belief

But for now

I let it be

For I must wait

Till turn of spring

To expunge the dregs

Of driveway tea.

FALL HAS FALLEN

My love loves

To kick through

Crispy crunchy

Maple leaves

Strewn willy nilly

Upon the ground

Oakie ones

Are okay too

Mixed with

Pixie caps

Atop acorn nuts

Green or nutty brown.

Fall may have

Fallen

But it doesn't

Get her down.

THE MOCKERY OF FALLING LEAVES

Their rustling skirts

Had quieted

Wherein before

They'd rioted

Across the

Concrete drive

There I'd done it

Seized the chance

After the wind

Had ceased its dance

Across the

Concrete drive

I'd applied some

Wind of my own

A regular

Hand held cyclone

Across the

Concrete drive

Now perfectly

Still and pristine

One might adjudge

"To the bone clean"

Across the

Concrete drive

But one need only

Turn his back

There'll be swirling

Leaves of no lack

Across the

Concrete drive

Drifting down with a

Clattering crackle

Triumphing o'er me

With a soft cackle

Filling the

Concrete drive.

FOR MY FRIEND JOHN

Hear Hear

Raise up a cheer

For this day

When John is King

Let all within this hallowed hall

His praises gladly sing

With an eye that's clear

 Undaunted

He trains his lens on one

 And all

He was there at the ready

At our every beck and call

No one ever charged

"Where were you when it counted?"

Though some may doubt

 His royalty

Or dispute the rank thereof

Why twas only yesterday

While we were in the pharmacy

When the man behind the counter

turned and said,

"Your prints, John!"

MY MIND

I lent

Someone

A piece

Of my mind

And he lost it

Should you find

My peace

Of mind

Please return

To lender

I'll think

Twice before

Ever again

I it tender.

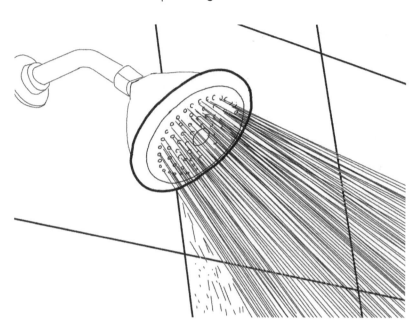

WHAT DOES IT SIGNIFY?

What

Does

It

Signify?

That the shower stall

You stand in naked

Once was driven down I-5

Upside down on the back

Of a flatbed truck

Even then

Closed to the world.

TIME RUNS QUICKLY

Time drips through our fingers

This side of the veil

But come the time we become

The best of ourselves

Resting the rest without end

In thankfulness blessed

With the Eternal One.

Other Haiku

or

Haiku Like

M D HAIKU

selfless and caring

to the helpless and growing

showing the way home.

(For <u>M</u>other's <u>D</u>ay)

A DAY AT THE BEACH

Diamond strewn glitter

Twinkling off and on again

Sparkling surf and sand.

SCREAMING RED

Screaming red

Echo shore

What he said

Poe no more.

SMUDGE OF SMOKY GRAY

echelon of trees

looking back at me

ashamed of their

winter nakedness.

GUTTER

Even a gutter

On a sunny day can break

Out in a rainbow.

SNOW HUSH

Snow folds its silence

Over the shivering trees

One can feel the hush.

The exact, appropriate word

LE MOT JUSTE

To use a wrong word

To worship the Word

Is in a word

Reckless.

MY PRONOUNS

Since you want to know

They are I - Me - He - Him - Who

And sometimes Hey You.

NOT A HURRICANE

Do not misgender

When you name it Archibald

It's a him-icane.

FOUND IN GOD

How long do we look

When we look to find ourselves?

Just be found in God.

OBEDIENCE

He who won't obey

Has found it far easier

To live in the lie.

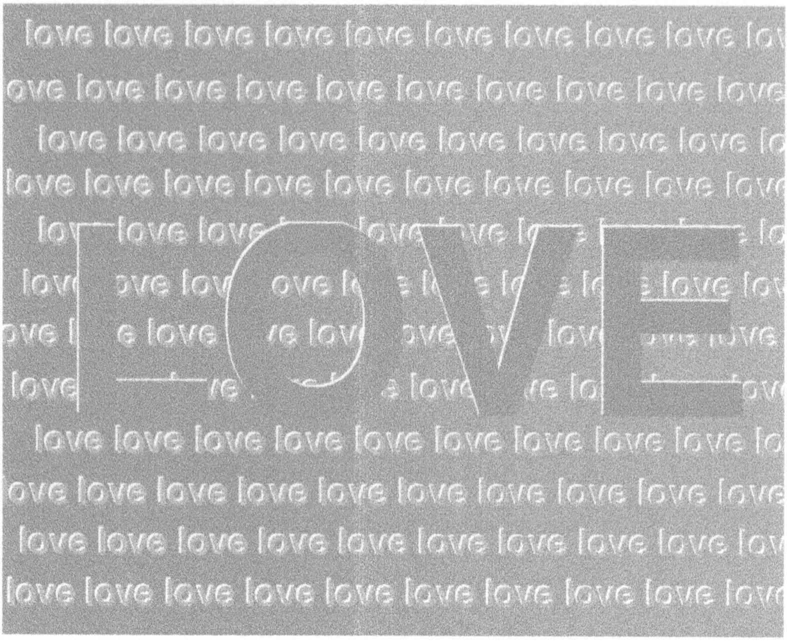
LOVE

LOVE LOVE

love - ours the feeling.

LOVE - His the doing, dying, living.

POURED OUT

A poured out heart now

Leads to fullness of joy when

He fills your parched soul.

THERE IS NONE

There is none, no none

Like unto the Holy One

Bred and bled for all.

CLOSING QUOTE

The Lord is my strength and song,

And He has become my salvation;

He is my God, and I will praise Him;

My father's God, and I will exalt Him.

EXODUS 15:2 NKJV

WATCH FOR MY NEXT PUBLICATION

COMING SOON

I am excited to announce that I will be publishing my third novel this fall, in September 2024.

It is the second installment in The Fairy Diary fantasy series. It is entitled Meribabell and the Crack of Doom. The Narrator picks up the story from the first volume translating the mysterious diary that he found under a cabbage in his garden. They are the further adventures of the fairy Meribabell and his fellow fairies Rumbletwist and Noralei, and their companion, the pixie Dunfallon. At the close of the first story the dwarvish outpost city had been freed from the Dark Elves who returned to the surface, having been freed themselves from the influence of the unknown Adversary. But things are still unsettled. War is in danger of breaking out between the two dwarvish kingdoms. And Meribabell and his friends at the direction of the High Fairy, and with the aid of Merlin are scouring the land on the hunt for the mysterious Adversary.

Look for the Barnabas Press page on Facebook.

Or my website: barnabaspress.net

ALSO BY THE SAME AUTHOR

OTHER TITLES FROM BARNABAS PRESS

by RALPH OSGOOD

The First Tuesday Poetry series

SONGS OF THE PROPHETS

BODY LIFE

FAMILY & OTHER HAIKU

(in your hand)

The Performing Arts series

PETER AND THE SERPENT

RUNNING OUT OF SKY

WILLIE & TAD'S PA

THE OutR daRk

The Fairy Diary series

MERIBABELL AND THE UNDEAD TROLLS

Coming soon

MERIBABELL AND THE CRACK OF DOOM

My Stand Alone Novel

DIARY OF THE END OF THE WORLD

ABOUT THE PUBLISHER

Barnabas Press

I created the Barnabas Press, registering it as a business in the State of Washington in May of 2022. It has always been my intent to select this title as a production entity. This springs from the time long ago when we were studying in the Book of Acts in the New Testament at church. During that study I learned about the man called Barnabas, who was a mentor and friend to the Pharisee Saul (who became the Apostle Paul). This individual was a Jewish Levite by the name of Joseph from the island of Cyprus. After his personal sacrifices to help the young church in Jerusalem, the apostles there gave him the special name of Barnabas - which has as its meaning - "the son of encouragement."

This defines the purpose behind my press. I am hoping to encourage my readers through the publication of my writings.

RWOz2

AUTHOR BIO

I am a poet, an historian, a novelist, and a writer for stage and screen, but foremost a responder to Jesus (Romans 5:8).

I was employed for over forty years in the entertainment industry, the last thirty of which I have crunched numbers successively for three of the top ten theater circuits in the US.

Back then my forte was numbers, added up in columns and balanced. Now I am hard at work exploring the richness of existence in a passion for words. Words that add up into poems, works of fiction and non, and works to be performed.

I am currently writing my fourth novel, looking out from my window onto the great Pacific Northwest, where I live with my wife Karen.

Join me as I follow the Word

Milton Keynes UK
Ingram Content Group UK Ltd.
UKHW020843030624
443491UK00013B/292